Christopher And Grandma On Safari

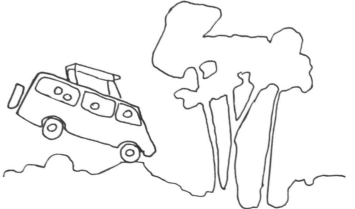

For Christopher

Christopher And Grandma On Safari

By Joan Barton Barsotti

Illustrated by Carol Mathis

Barsotti Publishing Co.
Camino, California

Christopher And Grandma On Safari

The day was just beginning at the safari camp.

Christopher had finished his breakfast and had

come back to the tent to get his camera.

He closed the zipper of the tent and tied it carefully.

He did NOT leave any sweets in the tent.

The baboons liked to hunt for sweets and could undo

the zippers if they were not tied properly.

He stood very still and listened . . . and then he heard them . . .

"Ooh-ooh, ooh-ooh, ooh, ooh."

The baboons were in the trees, just outside the camp.

Christopher looked down the hillside and saw the Masai.

He stood there, tall and regal,

his bright red cloth draped over his shoulder,

his walking stick at his side.

The Masai guarded the campgrounds every day and

stopped the baboons from entering the camp.

Christopher waved and the Masai waved back.

Christopher was sad, for tomorrow he would be going home.

"Jambo, Christopher." He turned and saw his friend, Moses, the camp manager's son. "Jambo, Moses," he said and almost smiled. "Moses, you look just like the Masai!"
"I AM a mighty Masai!" said Moses. Then he looked closely at Christopher and stopped pretending. "Ah, Christopher, you are sad because soon you must go home."

"But Christopher, have we not had a good time? Have you not seen many animals? And Christopher," he said, "maybe today you will find THE LITTLE BROWN GIRAFFE, the only one in all of Kenya! Remember what my father said. If you see him, you will return someday."

"Jambo, boys," said Grandma, as she came down the path.

"Jambo, Grandma."

"Jambo, Mama," said Moses. "Are you ready to hunt for more animals?"

"Yes, Moses. We are still searching for the little brown giraffe, the one they call Young Leader. Julius says today we will find him."

"Julius is the best guide in all of Kenya," said Moses. "The Masai Mara is very big, but Julius, he is very smart. He is waiting for you now by the van."

"Thank you, Moses. Do you think," said Grandma, smiling, "that you would like to go with us today?"

"Oh, yes! I will ask my father and I will change my clothes as fast as I can!" And off he ran.

Christopher and Grandma took their safari hats and cameras and went to find Julius. They had been on safari for many days. This would be their last drive and their last chance to see the little brown giraffe. Christopher was glad his friend was going with them today.

Julius was ready to go and so was the safari van. The top was pushed up and the windows were rolled down. When Moses arrived, they all climbed into the sturdy little van and off they went.

They drove onto the Masai Mara, the large game reserve. On the Masai Mara, the hunters only hunt the wild animals with cameras. Today they were hunting for the little brown giraffe. The sturdy little van carried them quickly over the bumps and around the trees.

They drove past a troop of baboons.
Some of the mothers carried their babies on their stomachs and as they ran
the little baboons held on tightly. "Ooh-ooh, ooh-ooh, ooh," they said as they
called out to each other.

They stopped to watch the lions and giraffes. While his family slept, the littlest lion cub pretended he was a big ferocious lion. He stared at a very tall giraffe who was trying to get a drink of water. The giraffe spread his legs out farther and farther as he stretched his long neck toward the water.

Each time the giraffe moved the lion cub growled at
him, and the giraffe would stop and stare at the littlest lion cub.
"Grr, grr, grr," said the lion cub. It took a long time for the giraffe to get his
drink of water.

They saw two very old elephants walking slowly together. Were they the
grandpas? Soon they saw a whole herd of elephants. The little elephants
ran and played together, but were never very far from their mothers.

They saw zebras and vultures, but no little brown giraffe.

Julius drove all over the Masai Mara while Grandma took photographs and Christopher and Moses looked for the little brown giraffe.

Julius stopped to talk to another guide. Christopher could not understand what they were saying, but he saw the guide point toward the bluff. Julius headed the van in that direction.

They drove near a river and saw the hippos in the water. They were big, and when they moved, they moved very fast. Christopher and Grandma were glad they were far away from them.

They looked across the river and far across the plains, but they could not see the little brown giraffe, the only one in all of Kenya.

It had been a long day and they were all getting tired and hungry. They wondered if they would get back to camp in time for dinner.

But Julius drove out farther and farther. He knew how much the boys wanted to find the little giraffe, and he knew he was there, somewhere.

Finally, they saw him! "Look, Christopher! Look over there!" said Moses. Far off in the distance, they saw a herd of giraffes going along the bluff. The giraffes were all very big, all but the leader, THE LITTLE BROWN GIRAFFE, the only one in all of Kenya.

Julius turned the van in that direction and off they flew, over the grass
and the holes and all the bumps in the ground. This was a real hunt! The
giraffes were moving very fast. Could Julius catch them? Faster and faster
they went. They held on tightly. Even Grandma held on with both hands!

Suddenly they were right beside the little brown giraffe! "There he is, Moses! There he is!" yelled Christopher.

The boys quickly scrambled to the back of the van just as the little giraffe turned his head and looked right at Christopher and Moses. "Wow!" they said, and forgot to take his photo.

When they arrived back in camp, Christopher and Grandma changed their clothes and hurried to the Dining Room.

Dinner was almost over when slowly the lights dimmed and the door from the kitchen opened. One by one the waiters came through the door in a long line, moving gracefully and singing. . . "Oie laleyio; Oie laleyio, Kamkampo."

"Look, Grandma," whispered Christopher, smiling, "now Moses is a cook! It must be someone's birthday!"

They watched as Moses carried the cake around the room, singing with the waiters, looking for the birthday person. . . "Wageni wetu; Wageni wetu, Kamkampo."

But the cake was for Christopher! It was not a birthday cake at all! It was a goodbye cake for a very good friend! And the two friends shared their cake with everyone in the Dining Room.
  "Oie laleyio; Oie laleyio, Kamkampo,
     Bye-bye wote; Bye-bye wote, Kamkampo."

The End

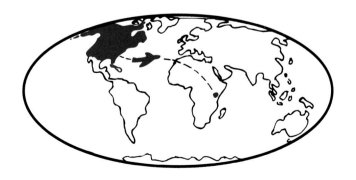

Learn some new words with Christopher

Jambo	- "Hello"
Kenya	- Independent country in East Africa
Kichwa Tembo	- Elephant's Head
Mama	- Polite way to address a woman in Kenya
Masai	- One of the many tribes in Kenya. The Masai are cattle-herders who herd their cattle on the open plains. (opt. Maasai) (mä´sĭ) (mä sĭ´)

∞ ∞ ∞ ∞ ∞ ∞ ∞ ∞

Traditional Goodbye Song

This is the Traditional Goodbye Song that was sung by the waiters.
It is a traditional Maasai song that has been adapted into Swahili.
The English translation is a loose translation and allows for the extra line.
Each line is repeated twice. Rhythm instruments can be used with the song.

∞ ∞ ∞ ∞ ∞ ∞ ∞ ∞

Oie Laleyio
(English Version)

Oie laleyio: Oie laleyio, Kamkampo

We are Kenyans; We are Kenyans, Kamkampo

Welcome to Kenya; Welcome to Kenya, Kamkampo

Welcoming you; Welcoming you, Kamkampo

To Kichwa Tembo; To Kichwa Tembo, Kamkampo

The Camp of fun; The Camp of fun, Kamkampo

A lot of happiness; A lot of happiness, Kamkampo

We love you all; We love you all, Kamkampo

We love to see you; We love to see you, Kamkampo

Welcome to Kichwa; Welcome to Kichwa, Kamkampo

A lot of Game; A lot of Game, Kamkampo

Bye, bye to you all; Bye, bye to you all, Kamkampo

See you again; See you again, Kamkampo

Oie laleyio; Oie laleyio, Kamkampo

Welcome again; Welcome again, Kamkampo

Oie Laleyio
(Maasai Version)

Oie laleyio; Oie laleyio, Kamkampo
Kira leKenya; Kira leKenya, Kamkampo
Kintoomon intae; Kintoomon intae, Kamkampo
Kira le Kichwa; Kira le Kichwa, Kamkampo
Kiata enchipae; Kiata enchipae, Kamkampo
Eitoomoni ntae; Eitoomoni ntae, Kamkampo
Enkampi eKichwa; Enkampi eKichwa, Kamkampo
Kebore osotua; Kebore osotua, Kamkampo
Kebore enchipae; Kebore enchipae, Kamkampo
Wootu mara; Wootu mara, Kamkampo
Kebore nguesi; Kebore nguesi, Kamkampo
Oie Olesere; Oie Olesere, Kamkampo
Kidua Kenya ake; Kidua Kenya ake, Kamkampo
Entushukunye; Entushukunye, Kamkampo

Oie Laleyio
(Swahili Version)

Oie laleyio; Oie laleyio, Kamkampo
Wageni wetu; Wageni wetu, Kamkampo
Karibu Kenya; Karibu Kenya, Kamkampo
Mwakaribishwa; Mwakaribishwa, Kamkampo
Kampi ya Kichwa; Kampi ya Kichwa, Kamkampo
Niya furaha; Niya furaha, Kamkampo
Tunawapenda; Tunawapenda, Kamkampo
Kuona ninyi; Kuona ninyi, Kamkampo
Karibu wote; Karibu wote, Kamkampo
Karibu tena; Karibu tena, Kamkampo
Lala Salama; Lala Salama, Kamkampo
Kwaheri wote; Kwaheri wote, Kamkampo
Oie laleyio; Oie laleyio, Kamkampo
Bye-bye wote; Bye-bye wote, Kamkampo

Other books available by Joan Barton Barsotti and illustrated by Carol Mathis

Mike And Nick And The Pumpkin Patch

Nana Gets A Cat

For more information about the books, quantity orders, or speaking engagements, please write to Barsotti Publishing Company, 2239 Hidden Valley Lane, Camino, California 95709. School queries also accepted.

Acknowledgements

I would like to thank the following people for their technical advice and / or help:

Catherine Barsotti, daughter, trip planner and safari companion; San Francisco, California

Gael Barsotti, husband and safari companion; Camino, California

James L. Brain, Professor Emeritus of Anthropology, SUNY New Paltz, New York

Chuck and Judy Loos, friends and safari companions; Newport Beach, California

Marilyn Barton Mezzarobba, sister and grandma; Calgary, Alberta

Deo Ngonyani, Department of Linguistics, U.C.L.A.; Los Angeles, Cailfornia

Bryan W. Payne, Resident Manager, Kichwa Tembo Camp; Masai Mara, Kenya; Area Mgr., Mara

Maurice K. Rubia, General Manager, Kenya Mystery Tours Ltd.; Nairobi, Kenya

Dwight and Barbara Stoddard, friends and safari companions; Camino, California

10 9 8 7 6 5 4 3 2 1

ISBN: 0-9642112-2-X (pbk) (children's fiction)